This Walker book belongs to:

_____

_____

_____

We lost HER!

PLEASE CALL US

~HELP~

We want to go home

ATTENTION,

Missing Cat Contact us

FIND MARMIE & PEA

MISSING CAT

REWARD OFFERED

SHOW ME THE WAY TO GO HOME
Have you seen her?

LOST

MISSING

LAST SEEN
REWARD $2000

Lost Cat....
please bring our Mae home!

LOST

SOCKS STEALER

LOST LULU

She is sleepy all the time

LOST PET

Daisy ♥♥

LOST CAT

COULD BE HIDING CALL IF SEEN!

LOST MALE CAT

3 LEGS

SOCKS STEALER

IF YOU SEE HIM

PLEASE CONTACT

Please Return

↑ He eats a lot every day.

MISSING

"Maggie"

IF YOU SEE ME

PLEASE TAKE ME HOME

MISSING FROM GARAGE!

HE LOVES FOOD REWARD

We are looking for her!

HAVE YOU SEEN HER?

LOST CAT!

She is Cali

LOST Chubby Cat

CALL immediately!

HELP!!!

PLEASE FIND

LOST

$1000 REWARD

MISSING CAT

Must Find Duchy!!!

LOST

MISSY THE CAT

REWARD OFFERED

$ 2000 !!

Mi Mi is

LOST!!

MISSING

MOMO

LOST

REWARD

Missing

MISSING FROM BACKYARD

$4000 !

LOST CAT

REWARD IF YOU

REWARD

I WANT TO GO HOME!!

Ernie male 2 years old

LOST GRAY MALE CALL

LOST!!!

BIG BLACK CAT WITH TWO WHITE TEETH !!!

~LOST~

LOST

HAVE YOU SEEN Muesli?

HELP FIND!

$2500

HAVE YOU

FOUND HER?

MISSING

OUT

MISSING

CAT!

HE DISAPPEARED

LAST NIGHT...

MISSING

CROOKED TAIL

HAVE YOU SEEN Our CAT?

Our dog is missing her!

LOST! -$$$$ REWARD

PLEASE HELP

LOST KITTY

LOOK AT THESE CATS!

REWARD 3000

To Toni, Harri and Charlie ~ M.R.

Harri　　Charlie

To all the cats in this book:

劃冰

Happy、Amber、高麗菜、王大吉. Face、阿咪、露姬、花花、吳妮妮、Neo、阿肥、Charcoal、廖妞妞、王咪咪、胖胖、Qtt、Chubby、王岱萌、摸摸、小Do、湯圓、白雪、Cofe、楊妮妮、小安、Amy、巴特、小胡弟、Choco、老咪咪、小咪、樂樂、蔥花、紅豆、阿蓮、Soap、Mumu、王雪飛、陳咪咪、芋粿、張小樂、Sally、罵收、Muesli、Ernie、Goofy、小乖咪、泱泱、咪吉、張咪咪、鳥咪、趴米、阿呆、南寶、奶油、歐歐、金金、Pussy、Tora、小葵、萌萌、小金鋼、咪嚕、卡栗、khaki、貓咪、瞎瞎、髒髒、乖乖、阿蒲、阿笨、Pandalin、綠油精、喇咪、芭樂、Klavier. Two、O₂、Maoma、呂小皮、小不點、豆子、三三、花花、雷弟、光復路、忌廉、tttt、苣苣、小叮、捲頭、該該、Miken、小豆姜、柚子、Momo、張有為、毛弟、莊毛毛、Fubo、龍龍、黑雪 ~ C.L.

First published in Great Britain 2019 by Walker Books Ltd, 87 Vauxhall Walk, London SE11 5HJ · This edition published 2020 · Text © 2018 Michelle Robinson · Illustrations © 2018 Chinlun Lee · The right of Michelle Robinson and Chinlun Lee to be identified as author and illustrator respectively of this work has been asserted by them in accordance with the Copyright, Designs and Patents Act 1988 · This book has been typeset in Filosofia · Printed in China · All rights reserved. No part of this book may be reproduced, transmitted or stored in an information retrieval system in any form or by any means, graphic, electronic or mechanical, including photocopying, taping and recording, without prior written permission from the publisher. · British Library Cataloguing in Publication Data: a catalogue record for this book is available from the British Library · ISBN 978-1-4063-8303-4 · www.walker.co.uk · 10 9 8 7 6 5 4 3 2 1

The Pawed Piper

Michelle Robinson   illustrated by Chinlun Lee

WALKER BOOKS
AND SUBSIDIARIES

LONDON · BOSTON · SYDNEY · AUCKLAND

I wanted a cat to cuddle.

A great big furry fluffball,
like the cat in my book.

So I laid a trail.

Balls of wool and
ribbon ...

saucers of milk ...

tiny balls
that jingled ...

and soft cushions.

Now, what *else*
did cats like?

I called in on my gran.

She said that
Hector liked catnip,

cardboard boxes

and helping to read
the newspaper.

I borrowed some things.

Then, I waited...

But no cats came.

Not even a kitten.

So I took my book to bed,
and hugged that instead.

Then something
woke me up.

Something purry,

something furry,

something warm

and soft

and cuddly...

"Hallo, Hector!"

"Oh, you brought a friend.
And another ... and another!

ALL
THE
CATS!"

Five, six, seven, eight ...
nine, ten, eleven...
I lost count at
SIXTY SEVEN!

Fat ones, skinny ones,
massive ones and mini ones.
Cats with spots and cats with stripes.
Grumpy cats with scowling faces,
playful ones that chased my laces.

But when I went to take
Hector home...

"Oh, no!"

I didn't mean to take
anyone else's cat,
I just wanted one
of my own.

Gran said I had to give them back.

ALL THE CATS.

It wasn't fair, everyone else had a cat to cuddle.

Me? I just had my book.

Although...

I'd forgotten about the cat in my sock drawer.

She'd been so quiet.

And now I knew why...

ALL THE KITTENS!
Black ones, cream ones,
somewhere-in-between ones.
Each with tiny paddy paws
and perfect elfin ears.

I loved them *all*,
and I looked after them
until it was time for them
to go to their new homes.

All except the smallest one,
who had made himself
at home in the corner
and wouldn't leave...

Not ever.

MISSING CAT
FOUND
Music and
Duchy!!!

Found !!

LOST FOUND
MISSY THE CAT
REWARD OFFERED
$ 2000 !!

MiMi is
FOUND
LOST !!

MISSING
MOMO FOUND!

LOST
REWARD FOUND

Missing
MISSING FROM BACKYARD
FOUND
$4000!

LOST CAT
REWARD IF YOU FOUND

REWARD FOUND!

I WANT TO GO HOME!!
E... FOUND
2 years old

LOST GRAY MALE
CALL FOUND

LOST!!!
FOUND!
BIG BLACK CAT
WITH TWO WHITE
TEETH !!!

~LOST~
FOUND

LOST FOUND
HAVE YOU SEEN
Muesli?

HELP FIND!
FOUND

HAVE YOU
FOUND

MISSING FOUND
OUT

MISSING
FOUND
CAT!

HE DISAPPEARED
FOUND
LAST
NIGHT...

MISSING
FOUND

HAVE YOU SEEN
Our CAT?

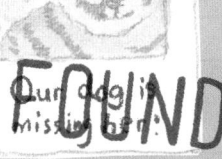
Our dog is
missing
FOUND

LOST! $$$$
REWARD
FOUND
PLEASE HELP

LOST
KITTY
FOUND!

LOOK AT THESE CATS!
REWARD FOUND

Photograph © Vicki Bunn

Michelle Robinson used to write copy for the world's biggest brands. Now she writes stories for children. Her picture books include *How to Wash a Woolly Mammoth*, illustrated by Kate Hindley, *There's a Lion in My Cornflakes*, illustrated by Jim Field and *Tooth Fairy in Training*, illustrated by Briony May Smith. Michelle lives in Frome with her husband, son and daughter. Find her online at michellerobinson.co.uk, and on Twitter and Instagram as @MicheRobinson.

Photograph © Hanshun Wang

Chinlun Lee, a graduate of the Royal College of Art, is the author-illustrator of *The Very Kind Rich Lady & Her One Hundred Dogs* and *Good Dog, Paw*. She is also the illustrator of *Totally Wonderful Miss Plumberry*, written by Michael Rosen. Chinlun lives in Taipei, Taiwan in a house brimming with all kinds of cat. Find her on Twitter as @chinlun and on instagram as @chinlun_lee.